Hamlet, Prince of Denmark

Sweet Cherry
Publishing

Published by Sweet Cherry Publishing Limited
Unit E, Vulcan Business Complex,
Vulcan Road,
Leicester, LE5 3EB,
United Kingdom

First published in the UK in 2012
2016 Audio and Hardback Edition

ISBN: 978-1-78226-337-1

©Macaw Books

Title: Hamlet, Prince of Denmark

Lexile® code numerical measure L = Lexile® 1040L

Text & Illustrations by Macaw Books 2012

www.sweetcherrypublishing.com

Printed and bound by Replika Press Pvt Ltd

About Shakespeare

William Shakespeare, regarded as the greatest writer in the English language, was born in Stratford-upon-Avon in Warwickshire, England (around 23 April 1564). He was the third of eight children born to John and Mary Shakespeare.

Shakespeare was a poet, playwright and dramatist. He is often known as England's national poet and the 'Bard of Avon'. Thirty-eight plays, one hundred and fifty-four sonnets, two long narrative poems and several other poems are attributed to him. Shakespeare's plays have been translated into every major existent language and are performed more often than those of any other playwright.

Hamlet: The Prince of Denmark. He is the son of the recently deceased King Hamlet and his wife, Queen Gertrude.

Ophelia: The daughter of Polonius, Claudius' trusted chief counsellor. She is also the lady-love of Hamlet.

Claudius: The new King of Denmark. He is the brother of the deceased King Hamlet, second husband to Queen Gertrude and uncle to Hamlet.

Laertes: The son of Polonius and the brother of Ophelia.

Hamlet, Prince of Denmark

Hamlet was the Prince of Denmark. He was away studying at Wittenberg when one day, he received the unfortunate news that his father, the king, had passed away. As Hamlet tried to come to terms with the fact that his father was no more, he received further shocking news that his mother had married Claudius, the king's younger

brother and Hamlet's uncle. Therefore, Hamlet had also been deprived of the throne, which should rightfully have been his after his father's death.

As Hamlet was preparing to leave for home, a strange event was occurring at the royal castle in Denmark. Th e guards had been complaining of seeing a

strange shadow at night, which resembled the dead king, and they were sure that the strange occurrences were the return of the king's spirit. After repeated sightings of the ghost over a couple of nights, the guards finally decided to inform Horatio, Hamlet's best friend and advisor.

Horatio refused to believe the guards, declaring that there was no such thing as ghosts and it must be a figment of their imagination. However,

upon their insistence, he
decided to accompany them
one night and, lo and behold!
he too saw the ghost of the
deceased king appear.

Horatio could not believe
his eyes. He tried to speak to

the ghost, but just as
the ghost tried to say
something, a rooster
declared a new day and
the ghost disappeared.
Horatio, now believing
in the existence of the
ghost, turned to the
guards and said, "This
ghost will certainly
speak to Hamlet!"

Hamlet returned
to Denmark and was
completely taken
aback by his mother's
haste to remarry, and
he certainly did not
approve of Claudius.

He could not
get the nagging
thought out of
his head that
his father had
not died a natural
death but had been murdered.
While lost deep in thought,
Horatio entered, accompanied

by the guards, and told Hamlet what he had seen. Hamlet assured Horatio that he would accompany them that night and wait for the ghost to appear.

Meanwhile, Laertes, the son of the king's chief advisor, Polonius, was getting ready to leave for France. His sister,

Ophelia, was in love with Hamlet. Though her brother and father consistently told her that she should not believe his claims of love for her, she paid no heed to their warnings, because deep within her heart she knew that he was madly in love with her.

Th at night, Hamlet, with Horatio and the guards, reached

the tower where the
ghost usually appeared.
As they stood talking
in the cold night,
Hamlet saw the spirit
of his father appear. He
tried to speak to the ghost, who
then beckoned him to follow. At
some distance from the others,
the ghost said, "Yes, I am the

spirit of your father. And the
reason I still walk the earth is
because I was murdered."

Hamlet gasped. He asked
the spirit to tell him more. The

ghost continued,
"It is being said,
my son, that while
I lay asleep in the
garden, a serpent
bit me; but the
serpent that bit your
father now wears
his crown." He
went on to explain
how while he was
asleep, his own
brother, Claudius,
poured the juice of the poisonous
herb Hebona into his ear,
killing him instantly.

It was morning
when the ghost fi
nished his story.

Swearing all those gathered there with him that night to secrecy, Hamlet decided it was time for him to act.

Over the next few days, Hamlet started acting rather mysteriously towards Ophelia. He pretended that due to

something troubling him, he had started to go mad. Ophelia informed her father about Hamlet's strange behaviour, and soon the matter came before the king and queen.

Polonius then made a plan to be sure about the prince's state of mind. He declared

that when Ophelia was with
Hamlet the next day, he and
King Claudius would stand
behind the curtain and listen
to what Hamlet had to say,
which should give them a better
idea of his mental problems.

As per the plan, when
Hamlet went to meet Ophelia

the next day, both Claudius and Polonius hid themselves behind a curtain. Hamlet said, "To be or not to be, that is the question: whether it would be nobler in the mind to suffer the slings and arrows of outrageous fortune,

or to take arms against a sea of troubles, and by opposing, end them." It was evident that Hamlet was talking about killing himself, and the king had heard enough. Claudius wanted Hamlet to leave for England immediately, sure that a change of scenery would help him to calm down.

But the next day, a group of travelling actors came to see Hamlet. They requested that he allow them to stage a play for him that evening. Hamlet saw this as a golden opportunity to nail his uncle and his mother for their crimes against his dead father. He asked the troupe whether they could perform the

play 'The Murder of Gonzago' for him. He also wanted to make some modifications to the original play and the troupe

assured him they would have no trouble in carrying out his wishes.

The Murder of Gonzago

That night, Hamlet kept a close watch on his uncle. Soon the play began. It started with a man sleeping and another man coming over to pour something into his ear from a cup. The man with the cup was the other man's brother, and had murdered his brother with the poison. As the play was coming to a close, King Claudius sprang from his seat and screamed, "Enough!"

As Hamlet and Horatio sat and discussed the matter, a servant informed Hamlet that his mother had sent for him. Since Polonius was not too sure about Hamlet's mental state,

he decided to hide behind the
curtain and intervene if Hamlet
tried to harm his mother.

On seeing her son,
Hamlet's mother at once
accused him of troubling the
king with the rendition of that

particular play. But Hamlet
also very subtly accused her
of being unjust towards his
dead father. His mother
pretended not to understand,
but Hamlet persisted. And as
she tried to avoid answering

his questions, Hamlet started to lose his patience. As his voice rose, Polonius, worried about the queen's safety, started to shout from behind the curtain, "Help the queen!"

Hamlet, thinking that it was Claudius hiding behind the

curtain, immediately
drew his sword and
thrust it through
the material, killing
Polonius instantly. Seeing
that he had killed Polonius
and not Claudius, Hamlet's
anger grew. As his mother kept

trying to divert his questions
about the death of his father,
Hamlet was preparing to kill
his mother when his father's
spirit appeared again. The ghost

asked him to spare his mother
and go after the real murderer.

Meanwhile, Claudius had
decided that he could waste no
more time in sending Hamlet

away, and so put him on a ship to set sail for England.

While in France, Laertes heard what had happened to his father and immediately returned to avenge his death.

He was furious with the king and queen, as they had made no arrests. He came back leading a riotous group of men, claiming that Claudius was not fit to rule over them, and therefore

Laertes should be their new
king. As he was arguing with
the king, Ophelia walked in. It
seemed that she had completely
lost her mind, unable to bear
the loss of her father. Laertes
was heartbroken to see his sister
in such a sorry state, and was
now more intent than ever to

avenge the death of his father
and his sister's state of delirium.

Now, while they were sailing
for England, Hamlet's ship was
attacked by pirates. In the fight
that ensued, Hamlet boarded
the pirate ship. His own ship
managed to break away and sail

off, leaving Hamlet as a prisoner to the pirates. However, when he told the pirates who he was, he was dropped off at the nearest port and returned home.

Upon seeing Hamlet again, Claudius started making plans for his death. This time he went to Laertes and told him how Hamlet had killed his father, Polonius. This infuriated Laertes and he wanted to kill Hamlet immediately. Claudius asked Laertes to refrain for a while,

telling him that he would
organise a sword duel. The plan
was for Laertes' sword to be
unprotected to allow him
to fatally stab Hamlet,
while Hamlet's sword
would be blunt
so as not to harm
Laertes in any way.

But Claudius did not stop
there. He also declared that
the tip of Laertes' sword would
be dipped in a special poison,
which had no antidote, making
Hamlet's death certain. Finally,
Claudius decided that if all
the other plans were to fail, he
would add poison to Hamlet's
drink, and the moment he took

a sip, his energy would start to drain and he would soon die.

While the two men were discussing how to kill Hamlet, the queen came running in and declared that Ophelia had

drowned. In her unsteady state
of mind, the girl had gone to
the banks of the river and tried
to pluck some flowers from a
tree, but while she was on a
branch, a portion of it broke off
and she went tumbling into the

river. She fainted as she hit the water and soon drowned. Laertes was shocked to hear this unfortunate news and could not believe his sister was no more.

Meanwhile, Hamlet and Horatio were walking towards the palace when they saw a huge funeral procession. It looked like a royal funeral, so they wondered who had passed away. Within a few minutes, Hamlet saw that the body being carried away was that of

49

Ophelia. He was shocked, and
could not understand how she
could have died. Hamlet could
no longer contain his sorrow
and went running towards her.
Laertes, on the other hand, was
furious to see Hamlet arrive on

the scene, and without another
thought, he rushed towards him
and grabbed his throat. Soon
they were involved in a struggle,
but with the help of the people
around them, they were parted.

Soon the king put his plan into action. He managed to convince Hamlet that Laertes had been named the 'best swordsman in France', and a match was arranged for the two men. Horatio tried to dissuade Hamlet, explaining that Laertes really was very good with the

sword. But nothing could make
Hamlet pull out of the fight.

Finally, the match began.
The king and queen were
also present, as were all the
courtiers. Even Horatio had
come to witness the spectacle.
As they started sparring between

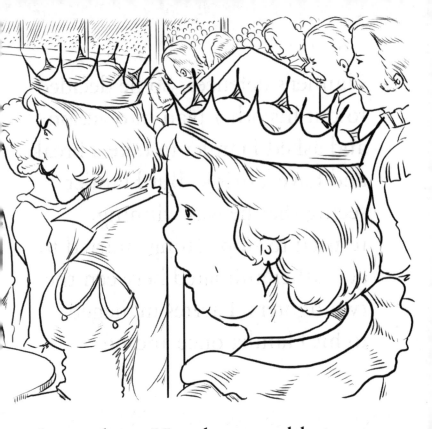

themselves, Hamlet was able
to get the first two hits against
Laertes. Claudius saw that
Hamlet was proving
to be better than
Laertes, as the
latter could not
even get past

Hamlet's defences. So he decided to put his other plan into action, and asked Hamlet to take a break and have a drink. But Hamlet, seeing that he was winning, refused to stop. Things started to get rather animated between the two fighters. Laertes managed to hit Hamlet once and he

immediately started bleeding. Realising that Laertes was not using a blunt sword, Hamlet became infuriated and started fighting with greater vigour. Little did he know that he had also been poisoned with that cut.

Since the fight had now been going on for quite some time, the queen was tired. Seeing a cup before her, she reached out to take a sip. The minute Claudius saw what was happening, he screamed, "Stop, do not drink that!" It was the poisoned cup that he had kept for Hamlet, but alas, it was too late!

Meanwhile, the fight was becoming rather

severe. During the match,
both contestants dropped their
swords once and, by mistake,
picked up each other's sword.
Now Hamlet, fighting with
Laertes' sword, was able to draw
blood from his opponent. He
was about to continue, when
he heard his mother scream,
"Son, I have been poisoned!"

Laertes too had fallen,
his own poison mixing with

his blood. Horatio exclaimed,
"They bleed on both sides.
How is that, my Lord?"

To this Laertes said, "It is
the king, Hamlet. He planned
the whole thing. He has
poisoned your mother. He has
poisoned the tip of my sword.

Nothing can save us now.
We are both going to die."

Hamlet soon understood
Claudius' plan. Without wasting
another moment, he pushed
his sword towards
the king, killing
him instantly.

Falling into Horatio's lap, Hamlet said, "I am dying, Horatio. But you live, and must tell my true story to the world." And soon he was dead.